Rose and Walsh

Neil Simon

A SAMUEL FRENCH ACTING EDITION

SAMUEL
FRENCH
FOUNDED 1830

SAMUELFRENCH.COM
SAMUELFRENCH-LONDON.CO.UK

MUSIC USE NOTE

Licensees are solely responsible for obtaining formal written permission from copyright owners to use copyrighted music in the performance of this play and are strongly cautioned to do so. If no such permission is obtained by the licensee, then the licensee must use only original music that the licensee owns and controls. Licensees are solely responsible and liable for all music clearances and shall indemnify the copyright owners of the play(s) and their licensing agent, Samuel French, against any costs, expenses, losses and liabilities arising from the use of music by licensees. Please contact the appropriate music licensing authority in your territory for the rights to any incidental music.

IMPORTANT BILLING AND CREDIT REQUIREMENTS

If you have obtained performance rights to this title, please refer to your licensing agreement for important billing and credit requirements.

CHARACTERS

ROSE STEINER – She is 64 years old. A pulitzer-prize winning playwright.

WALSH MCLAREN – He is in his mid fifties. A famous mystery writer.

ARLENE MOSS – 34, Rose's assistant.

GAVIN CLANCY – mid-30s. A young, talented, writer

ACT I
(SCENE 1)

(It's 1984. A beach house in Montauk, Long Island. The set consists mainly of the large living room, which is on top of a bluff that overlooks the ocean below.)

(A door at center stage, not the main entrance, leads out to a deck and then steps down to the beach. An entranceway at stage left leads to the kitchen, a bathroom and the front doorway, all unseen.)

(At stage right, there is a small breakfast area, which at present has a typewriter on it, scattered papers and books. There are bookshelves built into the walls that are overflowing with books. Below the book shelves are a couple of built in cabinets that are enclosed.)

(A spiral staircase leads to the upstairs and to the two bedrooms and bathroom, all of which are unseen.)

(There is a warmth and coziness to the house, lovely patterns on the furniture and lots of fresh flowers in the vases. It is anything but opulent. Probably bought 25 years ago when prices were sane. So although it is modest, it is quite attractive.)

(At rise: It's about two a.m. We can hear the ocean pounding against the surf from below. There is only a lamp on in the living room. Suddenly a woman appears on the staircase. She seems to be frightened, alarmed. She stops halfway down the stairs and calls out into the room.)

ROSE. Walsh? …Walsh, are you down there?

*(She comes down the rest of the way and turns the light on at the foot of the staircase. This is **ROSE STEINER**. She is wearing an old silk robe over her nightgown. She is 64 years old but with the energy and tenacity of a woman much younger.)*

(She opens the beach door and looks out. We hear the sound of the surf louder.)

ROSE. *(calls out to the dark)* Walsh? Where the hell are you? ...I need you, damn it!

(She leaves the door open, crosses to the bar and makes herself a drink. She downs it quickly and pours herself another one. She bundles her robe around her and sits in a big, soft chair, her feet tucked under her. She shivers, a cold flash surging through her body.)

*(**WALSH McLAREN** comes up the outside stairs into the house. He is in his mid fifties, lean, with short cropped grey hair. He wears a white terrycloth robe over some old pajamas and a pair of old tennis shoes. He closes the door and the sound of the surf diminishes. He has a quiet but quick sense of the sardonic.)*

WALSH. Was that you screeching like a banshee, Rose? I wish you wouldn't do that. You scared half a dozen turtles off their eggs.

ROSE. *(two hands around her drink)* I don't screech like a banshee. I'm a Jew-ess from Atlanta, not one of your Mick Irish barmaids from the Montauk Grill. Is that who you were rendezvousing with out there? Sitting on some turtle eggs of your own?

WALSH. *(He sits on the other side of the room.)* You're the only woman in the world I know, Rose, who wakes up funny...

(He puts his feet up on a table and sits back.)

ROSE. What were you doing on the beach at two o'clock in the morning?

WALSH. Well, Rose, there isn't a hell of a lot you can do on the beach at two o'clock in the morning. I was walking, I suppose, because the ocean wasn't half as restless as you were in bed.

ROSE. I hate it when I wake up and you're not there. God knows I should be used to it after twenty five years. Why can't you stay in bed until I'm up?

WALSH. Just to watch you sleep? Hell, Rose, we could hire a night watchman to do that.

(He takes a paperback novel out of his robe pocket, puts on reading glasses and opens to his place.)

…What are you so restless about?

ROSE. Oh, the usual trivia. I can't write anymore, I'm almost legally blind, and they took my driver's license away. Why are you sitting on the other side of the room when I'm so desperate to have you near me?

WALSH. I'll sit wherever you want. You call the shots here, not me.

ROSE. I don't want to call the shots. I want you beside me because that's where you'd rather be.

WALSH. That's not the way the game is played, Rose. When you summon up the dead, you accept the fact that we're nothing more than trained seals. I'm the entertainment, you're the impresario, babe.

ROSE. Oh, don't "babe" me, you smartass shitheel. You sound like a caricature of yourself that fell off the wall at Sardi's ten years ago.

WALSH. I was never on the wall at Sardi's. The last thing I'd want to do is watch people who go to musicals eating dinner.

ROSE. *(laughs)* Jesus, you're funnier dead than most people are alive. What are you reading?

WALSH. Pulp, honey. Pure crap. Reminds me of my early stuff.

ROSE. You never wrote a bad line in your life.

WALSH. Oh, I wrote them. My editor just never published them. But this kid's got the goods.

ROSE. You won't stay in bed with me, at least try to notice that I'm in the room.

WALSH. Well, I get lonely sometimes. Don't you know any other interesting dead people we could have over?

ROSE. Who? Louis Pasteur? Marcel Proust? Gertrude Stein? Are they dead enough for you?

WALSH. I need some nights off, Rose. This is a tough beat to pound seven nights a week.

ROSE. Then go. I won't stop you. I never could. I always hated the sight of your packed suitcase standing in the hall.

WALSH. Be honest, Rose. Some nights it was you who packed the suitcase and threw it in the hall.

ROSE. I didn't see any point in waiting for the inevitable.

WALSH. Then why do you waste these nights? Remember the good times. What the hell are you recreating all the squabbles for?

ROSE. Because you never walked out on me during a squabble. It's only after a week of love making that you and your baggage were gone in the morning.

WALSH. Well, that's true. A man usually makes too many promises in bed. Not that I ever intended to keep any of them. Hell, I always had to pay for my passion one way or the other.

ROSE. A twenty dollar bill on the night table would have had more integrity.

WALSH. You think too much of me, Rose. I rarely had the integrity or the twenty dollar bill.

ROSE. Still I miss you, you know. More than I care to admit. But you're a hell of a lot easier to live with now that you're dead.

WALSH. Well, fair is fair. I owed you a lot of happiness, Rosie. I'm paying off whatever I can.

ROSE. I'm not calling in your debts, God damn it. I'm just saying we could have had a lot more fun before you decided to have that aneurism.

WALSH. Sorry, I didn't expect a tire to blow out in my chest right in the middle of one of your dinner parties.

ROSE. *(She crosses to the staircase.)* I'm tired…Let's go to bed and see what comes up?

WALSH. You go on ahead. *(He holds up paperbacke)* I don't know where the kid is going with this thing but he's got me turning pages.

ROSE. "I'm tired" was a euphemism, you putz. Do I have to stoop so low as to ask you to accommodate me tonight?

WALSH. You never have to do that, Rose.

ROSE. What are you making such a fuss for? I'm the one who has to do all the work up there, anyway. There are some things that take more imagination than you can imagine… Please come, Walsh. I hate when we make love and you're down here.

WALSH. *(looks at her, hesitates, takes off his bifocals and looks at her)* …Rosie? Would you sit down a minute? There's something we have to talk about.

ROSE. Why waste time talking?

WALSH. Please sit down.

(She sits, he gets up, puts his hands in his pockets, and looks out at the beach.)

The reason I was walking on the beach tonight was because I was trying to figure out how to tell you some hard news.

ROSE. God, how I hate news from beyond the grave. What is it? You already died so what's the trouble now?

WALSH. Did I tell you it's my birthday in a few weeks?

ROSE. Of course I know. I'm not getting you a present. You never like what I get and how the hell would you return it?

WALSH. Do you know how old I'm going to be, Rose?

ROSE. I stopped counting at the funeral.

WALSH. Listen, I didn't even go to the God damn funeral.
I watched it from the bar across the street. I'll be 65 in
two weeks.

ROSE. We're past all this. I just want you to come upstairs
with me now and get into bed. You don't have to
perform. It's all simulated anyway.

WALSH. I was 60 when I died. At least I think I was, I didn't
read the paper that day.

ROSE. I don't care how old you are, were or will be. What's
your point?

WALSH. It's time for me to retire.

ROSE. What are you retiring from? Writing? You did that
when you were forty... Living? You got your gold watch
for that too... What are you going to retire from,
Walsh?

WALSH. From us.

ROSE. Us? ...What are you talking about?

WALSH. Even a memory has to move on. We've got two
more weeks, babe. No more personal appearances.
You'll have to make do with a scrapbook.

ROSE. Don't be ridiculous.

WALSH. Well, the fact is, what we've been doing all this
time is ridiculous... Thanks to your vivid imagination,
it seemed to work for us... But it's over, Rose.

ROSE. Let me clear up something for you, Mr. McLaren...
You come out of my imagination, not yours. You don't
come in off the beach and into my house unless I
open the door.

WALSH. Everything diminishes in time.

ROSE. Not as long as I'm holding the watch.

WALSH. How well can you see, Rose? How many fingers am
I holding up? *(He doesn't hold up any.)* You can't smell
worth a damn anymore. That's why you order half the
Botanical Gardens in here every day... You can't get
around here alone without your house guest up there
to help you from falling off the deck... How well can

you write these days? You've been on a book of short stories two years now that you used to knock off during the Christmas Holidays... Everything comes harder now, you know that, Rose.

ROSE. What I want, I can still make happen.

WALSH. Really? How many times do you have to call me in from the beach now? Three, four, even five times? The signal's getting weaker, kid. I used to be in here even before the name Walsh got out..

ROSE. *(looks at him frightened)* If this is some sort of cheap game, I don't like it. I'm not playing this, Walsh, you hear me? ...You are as real and as permanent as I want you to be. Now get the sand out of your hair and your sneakers and come to bed.

(She starts for the spiral staircase.)

WALSH. I'm trying to help you, dammit, can't you see that?

ROSE. Help me? By telling me I'm diminishing? I'm at the apex of my prime, kiddo. I lectured at twelve universities last year and some of the standing ovations I got are still standing... No, I don't bang out short stories as fast as brownie cookies anymore. I carve words out of granite now, so they'll stand like Balzac's statue for a hundred years... And that's not a seeing eye dog I have up in my guest room this week. That's my good friend Arlene, who is thirty years my junior and who is in awe of my indefatigable youth and vitality... Who are you to call me a fading rose when there are sandpipers out there picking at your remains? God, how I hate the impertinences of ghosts. Flaunting it in my face because you got through the ordeal of dying.

WALSH. I'm not questioning the eternal quickness of your mind, Rose. Just the inability of it to bring a buck into the house.

ROSE. I'm not interested in a buck. A young buck, yes...I have college boys banging on my hotel door at nights because they thought I still had a lot more to teach them than contemporary literature... At sixty-four, mind you... Two more weeks of you, is that all I've got? Well, you can get out now for all I care. No more bags to pack, that should make it easy on you... My God! At last. I'll have my nights free. You can't imagine how many invitations I turned down because I thought you might need me. A habit I got into during the last days of what you laughingly called your life...

WALSH. You know how that is, Rose. Some things, like writing or dying, are best done alone.

ROSE. Not for me. When I go, I want the Philharmonic Orchestra in my room. And a young Maria Callas singing *Madame Butterfly* and a few Gershwin tunes... And next to my bed will be the book reviewer for *The New York Times* humbly reading me the best God damn reviews for a life's work... When I go, I'll go in style. Not like you, who gave it all up when you still had something to give... Go on, Walsh. Take your bow and exit. In case you missed it, I just conjured you the hell out of my life. *(She starts again for the stairs.)* And quite frankly, sex with a dead man isn't half as good as I was led to believe.

WALSH. *(smiles)* Pound for pound, you're still the best in fighter who ever stepped into a ring, Rose.

(He crosses to the door. We hear the wind and surf again.)

(to **ROSE***)* If it's what you want, I'll leave now, Rose. *(He looks out)* Trouble is, I don't think they're ready to pick me up yet.

(We hear the sound and cry of a seagull overhead. He looks up.)

Well, if you can fly, buddy, maybe I can too.

(He goes.)

ROSE. He'll be back...he'll be back.

(A moment passes and **ROSE** *rushes to the porch door.)*

WALSH!!

(She rushes to the door, flings it open and calls out.)

Walsh, wait, you bastard! *(yells out)* Come back! Give me my two weeks. Give me what you owe me, you graveless ingrate....WAAAAAALLLLSHHHH!!!

(WALSH suddenly appears from behind the bar wiping his wet glasses with a napkin.)

WALSH. ...I do like the *Wuthering Heights* bit.

(She turns angrily and slams the door angrily.)

ROSE. What a cheap theatrical stunt... Well, you sold out to Hollywood before, it doesn't surprise me.

WALSH. We were all guilty of that one, sugar.

ROSE. Is it getting darker in here? I can barely see you.

WALSH. The lights are on, Rosie. Put on your glasses.

(Defiantly, she takes glasses out of robe pocket and puts them on. She looks at him.)

ROSE. You know why I don't wear my glasses around you? You're really not all that attractive at 20/20.

WALSH. When were looks ever important to you, Rose? You liked men for what they were.

ROSE. And what did you like about the two thousand odd women you've bedded since you were twelve? I bet you never looked up once. *(She inhales deeply and holds her chest.)* Christ.

WALSH. Are you alright?

ROSE. The dead worried about the living? Well, I suppose you people have nothing else to do...I'm fine. I just had the wind knocked out of me... You're really leaving, aren't you?

WALSH. So they tell me.

ROSE. Does this mean you'll never haunt me again?...Not even on Halloween?   .

WALSH. Nope. No tricks, no treats.

ROSE. I'll get over you. I've done it before...I'm just not good at being alone...as much as I hate admitting it.

WALSH. I always wondered who it was you had to be so strong for.

ROSE. I picked it up from you, Walsh. The only man born with two backbones... No, I was never as strong as you. I need people to love me, alright? ...Which is the surest way of never getting it.

WALSH. You haven't done too badly. You've had more friends, admirers, lovers and enemies than any ten women I know. They knew they weren't in your class.

ROSE. Don't dodge this one, Walsh. When did you ever tell me you loved me? When, in twenty five years?

WALSH. If twenty five years doesn't say it, I don't think you've been listening.

ROSE. I'm going blind, not deaf. Whisper it, just once, and watch my little ears perk up.

WALSH. You would really push me to say a sentimental line like that?

ROSE. I'm not publishing it, you shit. I just want to hear it.

WALSH. How much money have you got, Rose?

ROSE. You mean what's my total worth or how much do I have in my purse?

WALSH. I imagine they're both about the same. God knows you spend every penny that comes in... You've got four closets filled with four wardrobes and you still keep wearing that same black Chanel suit they've been waiting for at the Smithsonian.

ROSE. Never judge a woman by what she wears. It's what she buys that counts.

WALSH. You're broke, Rose. Between your doctor bills and fresh flowers every day, you're wiped out. And that doesn't include the dozens of charities you never say no to... Do you really think they're still looking for money to fight the Civil War in Spain?

ROSE. It's hard getting off the mailing list.

WALSH. You're going into bankruptcy, kid. How are you going to live? How will you pay your bills?

ROSE. I'll stoop to writing major motion pictures... Don't talk about money to me. When did you ever save a dime? ...You get your shoes shined and give the kid more than the shoes cost... People like me don't starve to death... There'd be a place for me at any table in town if I came in an oxygen tent.

(She starts for the stairs.)

WALSH. ...I know where you can lay your hands on a suitcase full of cash.

ROSE. I am not selling our love letters, which you never wrote in the first place.

WALSH. I'm talking big money, Rose. So big you could wallpaper the Montauk highway.

ROSE. You're serious, aren't you?

(He winks and smiles at her.)

...You are easily the most interesting deceased person I ever met... Alright, what do I have to do?

WALSH. Right here, in this house, in this very room, is a little bundle that could be worth a small fortune... Open the cupboard, under the bar.

ROSE. *(squints through glasses)* I'm looking. I don't see a cupboard. I don't even see the bar.

WALSH. *(crosses to it, points down at cupboard)* Here, for crise sakes. I'm pointing to it.

ROSE. That thing? I haven't opened that in years. I think it's where I keep my dust.

WALSH. There's more than dust in there...

ROSE. And I'm telling you I would never put anything of value in the middle of my living room.

WALSH. If you want it, Rose, you got to open the God damn thing.

ROSE. Don't yell at me. Instead of opening cupboards, we could be upstairs right now pretending to be screwing.

WALSH. How the hell did we ever get through twenty five years together?

ROSE. Well, we were apart for eight years and you've been dead for five years so it wasn't such a big deal.

WALSH. ...Is it asking too much, in light of the fact that I'm going to make you a wealthy woman, to bend down and open the cupboard? Just do it.

(She slowly gets down on her knees in front of the cupboard.)

ROSE. This better be good. I only get on my knees for very special occasions.

(She's on her knees. She pulls the little knob on the cupboard. It won't budge.)

It's stuck.

WALSH. Of course it's stuck. You paint over it every time a new color comes out... Just yank the God damn thing open.

ROSE. *(tries to pull it again but it won't budge)* I CAN'T DO IT! ...Why don't you do it? There's got to be something you're still handy at.

WALSH. I can't move things, Rose. I'm just a thought in your head and a thought cannot move inanimate objects... Oh, screw it. Watch out.

(He steps back, looks at the cupboard, grits his teeth and tightens his fists...and the cabinet doors open, by themselves. ROSE is amazed.)

ROSE. That is the sexiest thing you've ever done in your life.

WALSH. Cheap carnival trick. To think I had to die to do something like that.

ROSE. If you can do what you just did, we should rethink going upstairs.

WALSH. *(peers into the cabinet)* There it is, Rose. I can see it from here. A million dollars just sitting there. Hell, maybe three or four.

ROSE. *(She looks into the cabinet, takes out some old magazines.)* For a few old copies of *The New Yorker*? You think Sotheby's has gone completely insane?

WALSH. Keep looking, sweetheart.

ROSE. *(takes out a thin manuscript)* What's this?

WALSH. Forget that. It's not important.

ROSE. It's the introduction I wrote to your collected works. What do you mean it's not important? It's one of the best things I've ever written.

WALSH. We're wasting time and money, Rose. We're losing bank interest on what's in that cabinet.

ROSE. *(thumbs through her prose)* God, you were fun to write about. In forty-two years behind a typewriter, I never once invented a character as interesting as you. Your life intimidated all my fiction.

WALSH. Rose, I don't have time to listen to you selling yourself short. There it is. The brown package. Take it out.

(She takes it out. It's dusty, wrapped in brown paper that is faded, tied with a string.)

Alright, bring it over here. On the table.

*(He crosses to the table but **ROSE** doesn't rise.)*

What are you waiting for?

ROSE. I can't get up. My knees are locked.

WALSH. Come on, I said no more cheap stunts.

ROSE. I've been called everything but never a cheap stunt.

(She puts one hand on the cabinet shelf and pushes herself up with great difficulty.)

How do all those old Catholic women get up at Mass?

(She's up.)

WALSH. Bring it over here.

(She drops it on the table, exhausted.)

(WALSH *looks at the package. Walks around it gleefully.)*

There it is, Rose of my Heart. Your first class ticket to the bountiful life. We've got it, sweetheart, right in our hands. *(He looks at her.)* Why are you looking at me like that?

ROSE. Just watching the excitement in your eyes. How your silly, childish games exhilarate me. You're a hell of a man, Walsh, but you've still got a lot of boy in you... Let's not open it up.

WALSH. What are you talking about?

ROSE. Give it to charity...and give the next two weeks to me.

WALSH. Sorry, Rose, they don't do business like that... Open it up, sugar.

(ROSE starts to pull on the cord but it won't break. She pulls harder, to no avail. She's exhausted.)

ROSE. You always tied your knots so damn tight. It took me an hour to get your shoes off.

WALSH. Get a knife, for God sakes. Two Pulitzer Prizes and you can't open a package.

ROSE. The Pulitzer Prizes came in thin envelopes.

(She limps towards a drawer, takes out a knife. She limps back. She tries to cut the cord, to no avail)

It's impossible. It won't cut.

WALSH. It won't cut because you're using a butter knife.

ROSE. I picked up a butter knife because I'm legally blind.

WALSH. Legally blind means you can't drive a school bus, not cut a piece of string... Now listen. Bend the package in a curve, then slide the string off. You think you can do that?

(She picks up the package, bends it and slides off the string.)

ROSE. There. It's off.

WALSH. Tear the wrapper off...

(She glares at him, then tears the brown wrapper off. She reveals a typed manuscript.)

Look at the title page... What does it say?

ROSE. I don't care if it's the Magna Carta, I've done all I'm going to do.

(She tosses the script on the table.)

WALSH. *(points to title page)* Don't you recognize it, Rose? "Mexican Standoff" ...It's my last book, for crise sakes. Don't you remember it?

ROSE. How can you ask me that? It damn near killed you... You lived through tuberculosis and a World War but that thing finished you off.

WALSH. What would a new, unpublished, rediscovered Walsh McLaren novel bring in today's market? At today's prices? Not including paperbacks or a movie sale... Hell, you could add three rooms to this house just from the T-shirt sales alone... What do you say now, Rose, ye of little faith? How long do you think it would take to finish the book?

ROSE. Well, you've only got two weeks before the Seagulls start pecking on the door.

WALSH. I'm not talking about me.

ROSE. I hope to God you're not talking about me?

WALSH. Why not? It's just another 40, 45 pages. You could knock that off in a week with a little rooting from the sidelines. You wrote the second act of a Pulitzer Prize winner in six days, for crise sakes.

ROSE. I was 35 years old then. And I could see the keys on the typewriter... I can't think like you, Walsh. Nobody thought like you. They'd spot a phony line in a heartbeat. No, not me, Walsh. I'd sooner inform on my friends than plagiarize you. Why can't you write it? Just dictate the damn thing to me. Then I'll tell it to Arlene upstairs and she'll type it.

WALSH. Hey, Rose. Dead is dead. *(points to his head)* What was up here once went up in smoke five years ago. I can't create, recreate or procreate.

ROSE. Well, you strung that line together pretty good, so who knows?

WALSH. And that one line exhausted me.

ROSE. Don't you remember any of it? Didn't you make notes?

WALSH. No, dammit. I was too busy dying… Come on, think, Rosie. We're in the last lap of a relay race and I just need someone to pass the baton to.

ROSE. Let it go, Walsh. If we've got just two weeks left, the last thing I want to do is unravel a plot. Leave it alone, I beg you. Let it rest in peace.

*(**WALSH** looks up at her, his face lights up.)*

WALSH. Jesus, Rose. You've got it.

ROSE. Got what?

WALSH. The answer we're looking for… *(He takes the paperback out of his robe pocket.)* This kid…and the title of the book. "Rest in Pieces"…Now what would you call that?

ROSE. A cheap title. What would you call it?

WALSH. A divine hunch. I don't even know where this book came from. I found it in the pocket of my robe a couple of nights ago. Who would have put it there?

ROSE. Maybe it was a Christmas gift from the dry cleaners.

WALSH. *(He's walking around, excitedly.)* We have to move fast… Now we find out who – *(He looks at the cover.)* Gavin Clancy is and what he's doing now.

ROSE. Probably celebrating the one copy he sold. You want him to finish your book?

WALSH. Why not? He's facile but there's a writer in here someplace. He can be taught. He can be coached. He's going to write. You're going to edit and I'm going to sit behind you and try to cheerlead this thing to the finish line. In the next two weeks, the three of us are going to turn out the best piece of detective fiction this town has seen in thirty years.

ROSE. Only you can come up with stuff like this, Walsh.

WALSH. And this is the stuff that dreams are made of.

*(He flips through the pages of the paperback and laughs happily at **ROSE**.)*

(fade to black)

SCENE 2

(The next morning. About a quarter to eleven. It is a bright, sunny, cheerful morning.)

*(**ARLENE MOSS**, 34, wearing slacks and a T shirt, sits at the breakfast table drinking coffee, eating a bagel and reading* The New York Times. *She turns every page very quietly so as not to make any noise.)*

(The phone rings next to her and she grabs it before it can ring again. She looks up the staircase to be sure it didn't wake **ROSE**. *She turns aside with the phone and speaks softly.)*

ARLENE. *(into phone)* Hello?...No, she isn't. Who's calling, please? ...Mr. Fox?...From Delacorte...I don't know, she usually doesn't get up much before eleven...She did?...What time was that?...Really?...I didn't hear her. *(She looks up the stairs again.)* I think she must have gone back to sleep...Is there any message?

(She gets a pen and writes it on the margin of the newspaper.)

Mr. Clancy is in Quogue for the week and would be thrilled to speak to her... Alright...516...Yes...Yes, I got it...I certainly will...Oh, I'm sure she'll be pleased to hear that...Goodbye.

(She hangs up the phone very gingerly. Then she goes back to her bagel and her paper...We see **ROSE***'s feet on the top of the staircase but not* **ROSE**.*)*

ROSE. I'd be pleased to hear what?

(She starts to descend.)

ARLENE. That Mr. Fox from Delacorte is a very big fan...I hope I didn't wake you.

(We see her now. She comes down, wearing her 'morning' outfit.)

ROSE. Who is Mr. Fox from Delacorte?

(She crosses to the coffee and pours herself a cup, black.)

ARLENE. Aren't they publishers? He said you called him at nine fifteen this morning.

ROSE. Did I? God, I was hoping it was a nightmare. *(She crosses to the window and looks out at the beach.)* What did he want?

ARLENE. He said Mr. Clancy is in Quogue for the week and would be thrilled to see you. He left his number.

ROSE. Quogue? I was hoping he was in Tasmania.

ARLENE. You were up very late last night, weren't you?

ROSE. Yes...were you?

ARLENE. I went to the bathroom a couple of times.

ROSE. *(sips from her mug, still not looking at her)* How much did you hear?

ARLENE. You know I never listen.

ROSE. You're such a good friend. I don't deserve you... How much did you hear?

ARLENE. A little.

ROSE. How little?

ARLENE. ...Most of it.

ROSE. The truth, Arlene... Am I losing my mind?

ARLENE. Noo...I don't think so.

ROSE. Tell me what you heard.

ARLENE. I don't think I should.

ROSE. Why not?

ARLENE. It's–I don't know–too personal.

ROSE. It's about me, you idiot. It's only gossip when you tell somebody else, not the person who said it.

ARLENE. I know, but I shouldn't have been listening.

ROSE. We were screaming at each other, how could you not listen?

ARLENE. I don't know. I feel such a sense of betrayal to even tell you I was lying in bed up there listening to a very intimate conversation.

ROSE. You only heard half an intimate conversation. So it's only half a betrayal...and since I'm asking you to tell me only what I said, it wipes out my half.

ARLENE. I don't want to get involved.

ROSE. Why not?

ARLENE. Because I think you were wrong and he was right.

ROSE. *(glares at her)* That is a crummy thing to say to me. You never even heard his side.

ARLENE I patched it together. You fill in the gaps very well.

ROSE. Oh, you think so?

ARLENE. Yes, I do.

ROSE. I don't mind your listening but I resent your paying attention. And if you are, maybe I'm not the only one here who's losing her mind.

ARLENE. Are you talking about me or Walsh?

ROSE. Walsh doesn't have a mind, you twit. It's blowing out there in front of my house... Don't you have the good sense to sort out what's real and what's imagined?

ARLENE. I did. I don't anymore.

ROSE. Well, you're no help.

ARLENE. Exactly. Which is why I don't want to get involved in this thing...I'm not the only one who thinks so.

ROSE. Who have you been talking to?

ARLENE. Marilyn. My analyst.

ROSE. You told her about Walsh and me?

ARLENE. I didn't mention names.

ROSE. What did you mention?

ARLENE. That you were a writer and that he used to be a writer when he was alive.

ROSE. Oh? Did you happen to mention the names of the books and plays that we wrote?

ARLENE. No. Not one... I may have mentioned that you won a Pulitzer Prize.

ROSE. Two Pulitzer prizes. At least inform on me correctly, for God sakes.

ARLENE. I'm sorry. I shouldn't have told you I told her.

ROSE. Please. You're compounding the felony… What did she say about my conversations with Walsh?

ARLENE. She didn't raise an eyebrow. She said two thirds of widows and widowers in the world talk to their dead spouses all the time.

ROSE. Walsh and I were never married.

ARLENE. I think you're covered.

ROSE. Did you tell her it's been going on for five years?

ARLENE. She knows one woman who's been talking to her dead husband for forty-one years… And now she wants a divorce.

ROSE. Really? Why? Has she got a dead lover?

ARLENE. I'm sorry. I have no sense of humor about this.

ROSE. Why not?

ARLENE. I find it touching.

ROSE. What's touching about it?

ARLENE. …That he's leaving you in two weeks.

ROSE. Oh? You heard that, did you?….When he walked out and slammed the door.

ARLENE. I didn't hear the door slam.

ROSE. Of course you didn't. They only slam in my mind. Gives me a God damn headache.

ARLENE. Is it true? Is he leaving in two weeks?

ROSE. *(shrugs)* Maybe…It's going to be a long winter.

ARLENE. How would you feel about that? If you never saw him again?

ROSE. Healthier…and unhappier. It hasn't happened yet. And he's not going without me putting up a hell of a fight.

ARLENE. Maybe you shouldn't. Maybe you should just let him go, Rose.

ROSE. I can't.

ARLENE. Why not?

ROSE. He keeps me going. He keeps me on my toes and reminds me of what I'm supposed to be doing with my life. I still feel young around him...and wanted. Because, honey, they just don't make his kind anymore. His after life is my best creation and if keeping him means losing my sanity, I would consider it a fair exchange...No. He doesn't go without a fight.

ARLENE. *(shrugs)* Well, if you need help when the time comes, call me. I'm right upstairs.

ROSE. What would I do without you? I'm going to ask Walsh to bring Gary Cooper tonight. We'll double date.

ARLENE. I'd have to ask my analyst about that... What was the sexiest thing he ever did?

ROSE. He opened the cupboard doors.

ARLENE. Is that hard?

ROSE. If you're dead, it is... You said he was right and I was wrong. About what?

ARLENE. About you being broke. About wasting it on frivolous things. You do. Why do you have to pick up the check every single time we go to a restaurant?

ROSE. Because you're broker than I am. You haven't written a movie or a play in years. Why not?

ARLENE. Because they offer me garbage.

ROSE. They offered you two movies that grossed over forty million dollars.

ARLENE. Right. And they were garbage.

ROSE. Your lifestyle can't afford that kind of nobility, kid. So what do you think of his get rich idea?

ARLENE. What get rich idea?

ROSE. You didn't hear it?

ARLENE. I closed the door and took a sleeping pill when you said you were on your knees. I've got to draw the line someplace.

ROSE. We found the last novel he was working on "Mexican Standoff." Pretty damn wonderful, as I recall.

ARLENE. I never knew there was one.

ROSE. Every writer dies with an unfinished novel. It's some sort of affectation... He wants to get it finished and leave me the royalties. I'd be rich as Croesus.

ARLENE. That's wonderful.

ROSE. There is nothing wonderful in what a dead man promises you. A dying man, yes.

ARLENE. You're not going to accept it?

ROSE. Accept what? There are still forty pages to finish. He can't do it and I certainly won't try. He has, however, picked a ghost writer. I can't believe I said that.

ARLENE. Who did he pick?

ROSE. The first author he happened to find in his bathrobe pocket... A paperback scribbler who showed five lines of promise on page 287.

ARLENE. Wouldn't it be wiser to take your time and look for a first-rate writer?

ROSE. We don't have time. We have to finish the book before Walsh gives me the brush... Do you realize it's more embarrassing if someone heard this conversation with you than you hearing my conversations with Walsh.

ARLENE. Do you want us to stop?

ROSE. Why do you believe all this? My telling you it happens doesn't make it the truth. Why do you accept it?

ARLENE. ...Because I love the relationship.

ROSE. He died before you ever met him...

ARLENE. I know how he thinks. How much he cares for you...the sarcasm that goes on between you two with so much love behind it. Walsh is more alive to me than any man I've met in the past fifteen years.

ROSE. Don't you even know how lucky you are? You've got your nights free, to read a book, watch movies, indulge in meaningless but gratifying one night stands... My need is so deeply desperate...I'm a prisoner of my own romanticism, sitting here night after night with the Phantom of the Opera, who won't touch me, fuck me or sing to me.

ARLENE. No, but God, how you two talk.

ROSE. I'm so glad you're in analysis because otherwise I would recommend it.

ARLENE. If it's so tortuous to you, why are you so afraid of losing him in two weeks?

ROSE. Because I'm afraid I won't make it through the rest of my life alone. Having Walsh here is like putting up signs all over the walls. "Think" over my typewriter. "Stop" over the liquor cabinet. "Sleep" over my bed... "Truth" over my conscience.

ARLENE. That's my point. What wonderful signs to put up. The only signs the men in my life put up were "Goodbye" and "I'm borrowing your car."

ROSE. Have our lives been reduced to how good the sign painters we met have been?

ARLENE. I don't think your life has been reduced at all. I think you're one of the most fortunate women I know.

ROSE. *(looks at her)* Arlene...have you fallen in love with Walsh?

ARLENE. *(looks away)* If I have, you have no one to blame but yourself.

ROSE. That bastard! I knew I couldn't trust him.

ARLENE. Calm down, Rose. It isn't exactly adultery.

ROSE. He'll find a way.

ARLENE. I never should have told you. What a thing to be jealous of.

ROSE. Alright, I won't be jealous. But if I find your footprints in the sand next to his tomorrow, we'll have to have a talk.

ARLENE. Would you rather I thought he was a shitheel and not worth your time thinking about?

ROSE. No, you have better taste than that... Besides, it's not him you fell in love with. It's the picture on the wall I've painted of him. My God, this is that movie "Laura" and Walsh is Gene Tierney... What have we done to ourselves, Arlene?

ARLENE. This is not a crazy contest, Rose. And if it is, we're running neck and neck. Let's get off it.

ROSE. I can't. I have to call up this idiot scribbler and finish that God damn book... Do you think this book is Walsh's idea or my own mercenary invention?

ARLENE. Maybe a little of both. Another sign on the wall. "Survive." Call the scribbler. Finish the damn book, kick Walsh out of the house and let's both get a new start on life.

ROSE. You're right...Give me Clancy's number.

(ARLENE *hands her the paper with the phone number on it.* ROSE *looks at the paper.*)

ROSE. Quogue... That's walking distance from here...I think I'm being set up.

ARLENE. Call him. See what he's like.

ROSE. *(looks at paper and dials)* I know what he's like. I read some paragraphs this morning. Clever without style or originality...What do I say?... "Walsh McLaren asked me to call you...Yes, I know he's dead but I've been busy lately.." *(into phone)* Hello?...Is this Gavin Clancy?...This is Rose Steiner...Yes, the writer...I got your number from Delacorte...That is your publisher, isn't it?...Oh. Four years ago. *(to* ARLENE*)* I think Walsh picked someone who's deader than he is. *(into phone again)* Are you living in Quogue now?...Whereabouts, may I ask?... *(to* ARLENE*)* He lives over the train tracks... At least he won't be expensive. *(into phone again)* I know this will sound strange to you, Mr. Clancy...as it does to me.....but I have a business proposition for you... Well, I need some help on a book I'm writing... Well, if you must know, Walsh McLaren suggested you...He read your book, "Rest in Pieces"...Yes, I know your book came out after he died...Perhaps he received an advance edition... Look, if you'd rather not take a simple compliment... Would you like to meet me or not?...I'm in Bridgehampton...That's five minutes from you... *(hand over phone, to* ARLENE*)* I can't explain to him how Walsh read it...Should I just say I have a wrong number? I need a cigarette.

(WALSH *appears in the room.*)

WALSH. He's just nervous. He knows he's out of his league, that's all.

ROSE. *(to WALSH)* Then why don't you talk to him?

ARLENE. Me? I don't know what this is about. I was in the bathroom, remember?

WALSH. Tell him to come over. Have a cup of tea with him.

ROSE. Tea? He doesn't drink tea. He only takes stimulants with a needle.

ARLENE. *(backs away)* Oh, my God. Is Walsh in the room?

ROSE. No, Arlene. He is not in the room... He's in my head, manipulating me.

(ARLENE *backs away, looking around.*)

ARLENE. Should I go upstairs?

ROSE. *(into phone again)* No. Mr. Clancy?...Hello?...I thought you went back to bed...May I suggest we talk this out over tea?...Here at my place...Alright, beer will be fine...Can I put my assistant on? She'll give you directions...How is two o'clock for you?

WALSH. Not during the day...I barely see you during the day.

ROSE. *(into phone)* Can we make that tonight?...About nine?

WALSH. Make it eleven.

ROSE. Or eleven?...Yes, at night...I do my best work at night.

WALSH. *(teasingly)* Yes, you do, Rosie.

ROSE. Oh shut up.

ARLENE. He is in the room.

ROSE. *(into phone)* Fine...If you'll just hold on...This is Arlene.

(*She holds out phone to* ARLENE.)

ARLENE. Can he see me? Walsh, I mean?

ROSE. Yes. He thinks you're very attractive...Be of some help, will you?

ARLENE. *(takes the phone, still looking around)* Hello?...Mr. Clancy?...

ROSE. *(to* WALSH*)* This should work out fine, Walsh...He does about as much writing now as you do.

ARLENE. Do you know where Old Bridge Road is?

(ROSE lights a cigarette.)

WALSH. I thought you were going to cut those out.

ROSE. *(to* WALSH*)* Well, I'm cutting them back in again.

(She inhales and blows it out.)

WALSH. See you tonight, Rosie.

(WALSH leaves the room.)

ARLENE. *(into phone)* That's right...Number 207...Third house on the left...You're very welcome. *(She hangs up.)* Does he hear what I'm saying?

ROSE. You mean Walsh?...No, not anymore...Like Dracula, he's not fond of the daylight.

(We dim out.)

SCENE 3

(a little before eleven at night)

(ROSE paces, wearing a white woolen sweater and smoking a cigarette.)

(ARLENE sits, watching her.)

ARLENE. How long can I stay?

ROSE. Until Walsh shows up.

ARLENE. How will I know when he shows up?

ROSE. I get funnier...and more seductive...It's like flirting with the wall of your bedroom.

(She puts her cigarette out. The doorbell rings.)

No... That's not Walsh...There's not enough of him left to ring a doorbell... Let the paperback writer in. I'm going out to find my ghost... Lately he's been watching the ocean waiting for someone to come get him.

(She goes out to the beach.)

ARLENE. *(calls to her)* What do I say to Mr. Clancy?

ROSE. *(from outside)* Can I get you a Heineken?

(ROSE is gone and ARLENE goes off to open the door. We hear the door open.)

ARLENE. *(offstage)* Oh, hello...I'm Arlene...Won't you come in, please?

(GAVIN CLANCY comes in. He is wearing an old, rumpled sports jacket, trousers that hang too low, an open white shirt, no tie, and sneakers... His hair needs grooming and his face needs shaving, yet there's something attractive about him... He's in his mid 30's. He looks around, then ARLENE follows him in.)

ARLENE. Did you have any trouble finding the house?

CLANCY. I don't think so. I'm five minutes early.

ARLENE. Miss Steiner just went out to…to…I'm not sure what she went out to, but she'll be right back… Can I get you a Heineken?

CLANCY. No, thanks… She drinks beer?

ARLENE. No… She had me go out and get it this afternoon.

CLANCY. *(He nods.)* Do you know what this thing is about? This writing proposition?

ARLENE. Well, not really.

CLANCY. You just give directions how to get here.

ARLENE. To tell the truth, I'm more of a friend than an assistant.

CLANCY. She tell you I don't write anymore?

ARLENE. She did mention it, yes…. What do you do now, if I may ask?

CLANCY. That's what she said. "If I may ask."

(He looks at a row of books on a shelf.)

She write all of these?

ARLENE. Yes, she did.

CLANCY. So what does she want with some faded ex-writer who has one paperback on his shelf…if I had a shelf?

ARLENE. Well, I'll leave her to tell you that.

CLANCY. You're right. You're more of a friend than an assistant.

*(**ROSE** walks in from the beach. Sees **CLANCY**.)*

ROSE. Ah, you're here…Hello, Mr. Clancy. I'm Rose Steiner. *(She puts out her hand.)*

CLANCY. *(shakes it)* Yeah. You are…Even driving over I thought it was a gag.

ROSE. If you thought it was a gag, why did you come, if I may ask?

CLANCY. *(He smiles at **ARLENE**, then to **ROSE**.)* I could use the money. If I don't get a writing job, I could paint your house.

ROSE. My house never needs painting. I have a man from Sotheby's come out and do it every summer with a small brush.

(**WALSH** *appears from the beach.*)

ROSE. Hi.

CLANCY. *(looks around)* Hi.

WALSH. Yeah. He's just what I pictured…Some slob who dresses down to impress the natives that he's his own man… Reminds me of me.

ROSE. *(to* **ARLENE***)* Oh? Going to bed so soon, Arlene?… Well, we won't keep you, if you insist.

ARLENE. Oh, no. I've been up since dawn… Good night, Mr. Clancy. It was a pleasure meeting you.

CLANCY. Likewise… And thanks for the directions…I would have driven right into the Atlantic.

(She smiles and goes off to her room.)

WALSH. He's got the patter down perfect. Right out of the fifties… This could be our man, Rosie.

ROSE. Won't you sit down, Mr. Clancy?

CLANCY. *(He doesn't.)* Look, I'll be honest with you. I don't know why you picked me and what you picked me for…I've seen a couple of your plays, read a few books… You're uptown. I'm downtown. I don't belong up here… So why don't we just get to it. What's up?

WALSH. Gaudy little guy, isn't he? …Flatter him about his book.

ROSE. I was very impressed with your book, Mr. Clancy.

CLANCY. I didn't know there were still copies around.

WALSH. Ask him why he quit writing.

ROSE. Why did you give it up, for heavens sake?

CLANCY. I was a one book man, Miss Steiner…There's thousands of us out there…You throw a stone, make a ripple in the water and two years later you sink to the bottom…I just ran out of stones, M'am.

WALSH. *(slaps his hands together gleefully)* I feel like I'm watching a black and white movie. *(to* **CLANCY***)* What did you do after that? *(to* **ROSE***)* Sorry. Ask him what he did after that.

ROSE. What have you been doing since then?

CLANCY. Wrote a few magazine articles...Spent a year in a garage...I'm good with cars...Worked on a freighter hauling oil to South America and a short stint as a private detective.

WALSH. *(eagerly)* I did the same God damn thing, Rose. Private eye in San Francisco...Ask him if he ever—

(ROSE *puts up her hand to stop* WALSH. *He does.*)

ROSE. *(to* CLANCY*)* What if you had a really good idea again? One that appealed to you, one that would start up your engines again...One that would make not a ripple, but a resounding splash at Doubledays?... Would you be interested?

WALSH. He'll bite at that one, honey.

CLANCY. If it didn't happen after four years on a freighter, it's not gonna happen here.

WALSH. Yes, but it might in Bridgehampton. Tell him.

ROSE. Yes, but it might in Bridgehampton...I would have finished the book but my eyes started to go bad.

WALSH. I'm asking you to be my eyes, Mr. Clancy.

ROSE. I'm asking you to be my eyes, Mr. Clancy... *(to* WALSH*)* I can do this myself.

CLANCY. I know you can.

WALSH. Give him the book, for Christ sake...

(ROSE *jumps up, glares at* WALSH *with her fists clenched.*)

CLANCY. Did I say something wrong?

ROSE. No. I get back spasms...from time to time... *(offers him the book)* Why don't you read it? Tell me what you think? I took off the title page. I don't want to intimidate you by seeing my name on it.

CLANCY. *(He smiles, enjoying her.)* Sure, why not?...I'll take it home and call you tomorrow.

WALSH. Tomorrow's too late. We only have two weeks.

ROSE. *(to* WALSH*)* I know that.

CLANCY. What?

ROSE. I know that the publisher will be calling me. I must have the book in two weeks.

CLANCY. In two weeks? Why?

ROSE. *(to WALSH)* Why?

WALSH. So that they can get the book out for Christmas.

ROSE. Because they want the book out for Christmas.

CLANCY. Why? They already have too many books out at Christmas.

WALSH. *(right into CLANCY's face)* It's a winter book, you God damn idiot...I'm giving you a break just letting you read it.

(He looks at ROSE, then moves away.)

ROSE. *(to CLANCY)* It's what they call a winter read...Heavy enough to keep you warm and smart enough to keep you from going for a swim.

(She looks at WALSH, smiles triumphantly.)

CLANCY. If you say so... How many pages have to be finished?

WALSH. The book is over when it's over...When you say to yourself, "God damn it, I did it."

ROSE. It's over when I say to myself, "God damn it, Rose. You did it."

WALSH. *(right at ROSE)* I did it. Me. Don't forget that, Rosie.

CLANCY. If I work on it, don't I get a credit.

ROSE. Yes.

WALSH. No.

ROSE. Maybe.

CLANCY. Which is it?

WALSH. It's only the last forty pages...Two author books never make a dime.

ROSE. Isn't it enough you'll be well paid?

CLANCY. *(smiles at her)* Yeah. It'll be enough... So when do I read it?

ROSE. Now. In here... I'm going to bed.

(She starts for the stairs.)

CLANCY. I read quickly. What do I do when I finish?

WALSH. Read it again.

ROSE. Read it again...

CLANCY. I didn't even read my own book twice.

WALSH. Maybe that's why your stones sank to the bottom.

ROSE. Perhaps that's why your stones sank to the bottom. *(She smiles, raises her eyebrows to* **WALSH**.*)* Good night, Mr. Clancy. I'll see you in the morning. *(to* **WALSH***)* Coming up?

CLANCY. What was that?

ROSE. They say a storm is coming up. It's the perfect time to read a book.

(She starts up the winding staircase.)

WALSH. *(to* **ROSE***)* I'm not coming up, I'm going to stay right here and see that he doesn't skip pages.

ROSE. I said come up!

(She looks at **CLANCY***, who looks back at her.)*

Come up, come up, oh storm of the sea...Ah brich oh brawning, a brook on the glee...Robert Burns...You've read him, I'm sure.

CLANCY. Maybe after I finish this book.

(She starts up the stairs... **WALSH** *starts after her, unwillingly.)*

You mind if I have a beer or two? You have Heineken?

ROSE. *(on the stairs)* Heineken is the only thing I drink.

WALSH. *(as he follows her up the stairs)* No fooling around tonight, Rosie... We have him on the hook. And when he bites, we pull together.

ROSE. Oh, God, I love it when you talk like that.

(They are both gone. **CLANCY** *crosses into the kitchen, opens fridge, takes out two Heineken, opens one, lies down on sofa and starts to read the book from page one.)*

(Lights dim out.)

SCENE 4

(Early morning. The sun peers into the house. **CLANCY**
is asleep on the sofa, the book opened across his chest.)

*(***WALSH*** *comes quietly down stairs. He looks around
making sure no one is around, then he walks behind the
sofa and leans over* **CLANCY***'s head.)*

WALSH. ...Listen, you little son of a bitch...If you screw this
up, I'll bury you...I know people who can arrange to
have you in pain long after you're dead...I found you
in my pocket, I can just as soon have you disappear
twenty miles under the Titanic...

*(***ARLENE*** *comes out carrying a tray with hot coffee, a
bagel and scrambled eggs.)*

*(She puts it on the small table near the sofa and looks
at him for a moment. He crosses his arms over his chest,
probably feeling cold.)*

*(She takes off her cardigan sweater and puts it over
him...then leaves.)*

*(***WALSH*** *turns back to* **CLANCY***.)*

WALSH. Rose doesn't want this book finished...She doesn't
want someone's fingers leaving marks on my legacy...
Are you listening to me?...She'll sabotage you...She'll
fight you to the death not to get my book published...
She's smart...Smarter than you and occasionally
smarter than me...

*(***CLANCY*** *turns in his sleep.)*

Don't turn away from me, you little shit...I can have
your testicles removed while you're sleeping....Don't
let her back you down...Stand up for my rights...

ROSE. *(voice from upstairs)* WALSH!!...Who are you talking
to?

*(***WALSH*** *straightens up, surprised that he's been caught.)*

ROSE. What are you doing down there?

WALSH. I...I'm looking through the cabinet...Maybe I left some loose pages in there...

(Then it's quiet...he goes back to CLANCY.*)*

See?...She's on top of everything... She'll trample you into dust with her Ferragamo heels... She's a skinny broad but she can break your back with an innuendo... If she wins, Clancy boy, my book goes to the pauper's grave with her...And she'll end up eating her own flowers... I kid you not.

ROSE. *(voice from upstairs)* Stop saying "I kid you not"... You're better than that.

WALSH. *(crosses to the stairs but calls back to* CLANCY*)* ...Get to work, you little bastard...I can feel my battery running down now...

*(*WALSH *disappears up the stairs.* ARLENE *comes back in to see if* CLANCY *is awake.)*

CLANCY. *(his eyes still closed)* What time is it?

ARLENE. Oh. You're up.

CLANCY. I didn't say I was up. I just asked what time it was.

ARLENE. *(looks at her watch)* A quarter to seven...I put some breakfast on the table for you.

CLANCY. *(starts to sit up)* You always get up this early?

ARLENE. Sometimes earlier. I'm not a good sleeper.

CLANCY. I could teach you how. You've got my number. *(He sits up, looks at her.)* ...What?

ARLENE. Nothing...It just sounded a little inappropriate to me.

CLANCY. Well, it's a quarter to seven in the morning... *(He picks up coffee.)* Are you just visiting her or do you live with her?

ARLENE. I stay with her. For the summer.

CLANCY. I see. You stay with her... What's in it for you?

ARLENE. I don't understand.

CLANCY. Sure you do. What's in it for you?

ARLENE; Friendship.

CLANCY; Don't you have any men friends you could stay with for the summer?

(She glares at him. He breaks off some bagel.)

What?...Another inappropriate remark?

ARLENE. Well, most of them seem to be...She's my closest friend. I've known her for years.

CLANCY. How close does it get?

ARLENE. If you hand me your cup of coffee, I'd be glad to throw it in your face.

CLANCY. It wouldn't be the first time...This is my third set of eyebrows.

ARLENE, Why are you taunting me?

CLANCY. Just seeing how far I can go.

ARLENE. Well, you can go back to Quogue as far as I'm concerned. *(She starts to go.)*

CLANCY. Nah, I don't think so. She's up there waiting to hear what I thought of the book... I also saw you looking at me while I slept... Is that why you brought me breakfast?

ARLENE. No. We're just civilized around here.

CLANCY. Yeah, I heard that about Bridgehampton. That's why I stay in Quogue.

ARLENE. Look, I don't have time to trade petty banter with you. I have better things to do.

CLANCY. Like what? What better things do you have to do?...If I may ask.

ARLENE. I'm writing a screenplay at the moment.

CLANCY. Oh. You're a writer... This place is lousy with them...Do I get to read your screenplay too?

ARLENE. Mr. Clancy, I think you woke up on the wrong side of the couch.

CLANCY. No. I usually wake up on the floor.

ARLENE. I can see why...

(She picks up the two empty beer bottles.)

...The gutter would be more appropriate.

CLANCY. Yeah, I know…I'm pretty seedy in the morning…I like your legs, if that's not too inappropriate.

ARLENE. Are you expecting a response to that?

CLANCY. It wasn't a crack. It's right here in the book. *(He opens the book, turns the pages, then stops and reads)* Here… Jake says to Madge, "I'm pretty seedy in the morning…I like your legs, if that's alright to say." … Written right here by the master.

ARLENE. Yes. She's a very great writer.

CLANCY. That may be so… But she didn't write this…Walsh McLaren did…By the way, there's dust on the pages. *(He blows the dust out.)* How long has it been sitting around this house?

ARLENE. I don't know what you're talking about.

CLANCY. Well, I didn't say it was a conspiracy but something's fishy around here… She gets me here to ask if I would help her finish a book of hers… Except this isn't hers… I've read every Walsh McLaren story ever written… He puts his mark on every page like the numbers on a treasury bill… Only I've never seen this book before…So why is she doing this?

ARLENE. I don't know. I only give directions.

(from upstairs)

ROSE. I'll explain, Mr. Clancy, if I can get my eyes open first.

(She starts down the staircase, holding the rail for guidance… She is dressed in a smart summer suit.)

Good morning… I hope you read well.

CLANCY. Very well, thank you… You always wake up in a smart suit?

ROSE. I think so. I don't really know how… I think angels dress me in the morning… Arlene, dear, would you pour a cup of that fragrant coffee for me.

ARLENE. Good morning, Rose. You look very nice… *(She gets a cup from the shelf and pours coffee for **ROSE**.)*

ROSE. Thank you, I'm lecturing at Stonybrook at nine.

ARLENE. Oh, really?

ROSE. Yes. This shouldn't take long. *(to* **CLANCY***)* You're quite right… It's Walsh's book. Not mine…I confess…I didn't quite think I'd be able to keep it a secret for long.

(She takes the coffee.)

CLANCY. And you're trying to pass it off as your own? I don't think so….Any publisher over forty-five would spot this in a minute.

ROSE. You're so clever… I'll bet you never spilled a drop of oil from that freighter… Of course I'm not trying to pass it off as mine… It will have his name on it and his name only… It's his name that will sell the book.

CLANCY. Where'd you get it, if I may ask?

(He and **ARLENE** *look at each other.)*

ROSE. It's been in that cupboard for over five years. As a gift to me…We were very good friends.

CLANCY. Why'd he leave you an unfinished book?

ROSE. Well, unfortunately he died on the patio… Still, I thought it was a beautiful gesture.

CLANCY. Well, friends or not, you're going to need proof he left it to you… His estate would want verification, otherwise you and I will have to defend ourselves in a courtroom… although we might be able to finish it in prison.

ROSE. I am the executor of his estate… And the sole owner of all his copyrights… I'll show them to you when I'm able to climb the stairs again.

CLANCY. And who would publish it? If the public finds out it was ghost written, they'll stay away from it like the plague.

ROSE. What if I told you that as you and I work on those last forty pages, it will still have Walsh McLaren's hand on it.

CLANCY. From the grave or do you keep it in the house?

ROSE. You lack tact, among other things… He left me copious notes on how the book should be finished.

CLANCY. Did he do that on the patio as well?

ROSE. Don't you dare be disrespectful to one of America's great literary figures.

CLANCY. I was out of line… Slap me any time you like.

ROSE. Maybe after lunch.

CLANCY. May I see the notes?

ROSE. They're not on paper. They're in my head.

CLANCY. May I see your head? …It was over five years ago. You don't remember how you got dressed but you remember copious notes regarding a dusty book that looks like it hasn't been open since I went to college.

ROSE. I never would have thought you did… And where did you go?

CLANCY. William and Mary.

ROSE. Did you finish?

CLANCY. Just William… So if your notes are not on paper and not in your head, where do we look?

ROSE. They're not easily remembered. I need you to pry them out for me.

CLANCY. Maybe we need a dentist instead of a writer.

(He laughs. No one else does.)

Were you a good friend of McLaren's?

ROSE. I feel as if he's still in this house… Arlene can tell you.

CLANCY. Okay, Arlene. Tell me.

ARLENE. Well, he had a very strong personality…Sometimes you feel he's standing right next to you.

CLANCY. Did you know him?

ARLENE. No. It filters down through Rose.

ROSE. Arlene is overly dramatic… The book, however, is mine. If you work on it with me, and we complete it, I'll give you ten percent of my royalties.

CLANCY. There must be something about me that you like...or need... So if I got my foot in the door, I'll push it open. How about fifty percent?

ROSE. You are not even worth ten. If I were you, I'd take my offer and buy yourself a garage in Quogue.

CLANCY. A new book by Walsh McLaren is worth half the beach front in Quogue. You made your offer, I made mine.

ROSE. I see... Well, you know where the door is, Clancy. Good luck on the rest of your shattered career.

CLANCY. *(shrugs, smiles)* Suits me...and thanks for the beer. *(to* ARLENE*)* The crack about your legs still goes.

(He turns and leaves.)

WALSH. *(from the stairs)* Don't let him go, for crise sakes. We don't have time to negotiate.

ROSE. I'll be damned if I let him swindle me and belittle you.

ARLENE. Do we have company again?

WALSH. *(to* ROSE*)* Tell her to get him back. Let's hear what he has to say about the book first.

ROSE. I couldn't care less what he has to say. He's an insult to both of us...I don't think he could write his way out of an open elevator.

ARLENE. Well, I think I'll mosey along.

(She goes.)

WALSH. Call him, Rose, or I'm out of here on the next seagull, I kid you not.

ROSE. I can take care of myself.

WALSH. The hell you can. Stop being a God damn martyr. What will it get you?

ROSE. Respect from my peers. I think your seagull is waiting.

WALSH. There's plenty of people waiting for you to fall, Rose. You'll make them very happy.

(He goes.)

ROSE. ARLENE!! Get Clancy back.

ARLENE. *(rushes in)* Is that what Walsh wants?

ROSE. Walsh is dead...again. It's my idea. Everything he says is my idea...Go get him...Now!

ARLENE. *(rushing off)* Mr. Clancy!

(WALSH appears on the stairs.)

WALSH. Everything you say is not your idea...I still can get through to you...I may need a pick and shovel to get there, but don't underestimate me, dead or alive.

(ARLENE rushes back in.)

ARLENE. He's coming...

WALSH. Take it easy with him, Rosie.

ROSE. Don't tell me what to do.

ARLENE. Did Walsh just say something?

ROSE. I am not your translator, Arlene...He said, "Take it easy on him"...

(CLANCY walks in, a cigarette in his mouth.)

CLANCY. I thought I'd get a call back.

ROSE. Don't be cocky with me. And put out that cigarette. It still doesn't make you look like a writer.

CLANCY. How about leather patches on my cigarette?

ROSE. Tell me what you thought of the book.

CLANCY. A little out-dated but no one writes that good today...What's the title?

ROSE. "Mexican Standoff."

CLANCY. Perfect. No one's alive at the finish.

ROSE. We don't know what the finish is.

CLANCY. It was a suggestion.

WALSH. *(sitting on steps of staircase)* Not bad. He's ahead of us, Rose...We either change the title or the finish.

ROSE. Arlene, get some booze... A large glass of bourbon for me.

CLANCY. I'll stick with the Heineken.

WALSH. I'll have the same wine I had with the poached bass.

ROSE. Get your pad, Arlene. Take some notes... Eavesdropping on nothing is pointless.

(She turns and goes.)

CLANCY. So what's with you two?

ROSE. Which two?

CLANCY. You and her...Why? Did I miss anyone?

ROSE. Arlene and I are not lovers, if that's what you think. And I don't give a damn what you think.

CLANCY. No offense... But she does jump through hoops whenever you want her to. So I thought...you know. Gertrude Stein and Alice.

ROSE. Gertrude Stein and Alice weren't lovers either... They were just in the same outfit in the first World War...

*(**ARLENE** returns.)*

Tell me what you think the book is about.

CLANCY. *(sits on the sofa)* Deceit...Two people who never said an honest word to each other... "Mexican Standoff."

WALSH. So far so good.

ROSE. I don't agree at all. There is no deceit. They're simply incapable of telling the truth.

CLANCY. Comes to the same thing.

ROSE. The hell it does. Not being able to tell the truth is an ailment. Deceit is not telling the truth to gain advantage.

CLANCY. Still comes to the same thing.

WALSH. Jesus Christ, can we get to the book, please?

ROSE. *(to **WALSH**)* What the hell do you think I'm doing?

CLANCY. I don't know. You asked me to tell you what the book was about and I told you.

ROSE. Who are you to tell me what Walsh McLaren's book is about? What do you know of his depth, his profundity, his instinct for taking the mundane and curling it around his brain and turning it into rhythmic, enigmatic and hilarious puzzles that would take a Rhodes Scholar a year to unravel? *(She opens the book, turns pages.)* Here... How about this?

WALSH. Don't fight him, Rose. Help him.

ROSE. Oh, shut up.

CLANCY. I couldn't get the floor away from you if I tried.

ROSE. *(reads from book)* 'His being a side of me was alright, of course, since everybody, is in some degree an aspect of everybody else or how would anybody else ever hope to understand anything about anyone else'

CLANCY. Well, that's pretty straight forward.

ROSE. My ass, kid. It's prose.

WALSH. That's not the way to collaborate, Rose.

CLANCY. I really don't think this is the way to collaborate.

WALSH. What did I tell you?

CLANCY. You just can't take something out of context and—

ROSE. Walsh never wrote anything out of context.

WALSH. Oh, don't start in with him again, Rose. Hear him out.

ROSE. *(to WALSH)* Will you let me handle this?

CLANCY. Do you always practice everything you're going to say?

ROSE. Yes. That's how I avoid rewriting.

CLANCY. Look, Walsh doesn't give the slightest hint about where the book is going—

WALSH. That's called 'style,' kid.

CLANCY. Or maybe he just got stuck.

ROSE. Never in his life. He's unstuckable.

WALSH. ...No. He's right. That was the page that sent me into a ten day drunk.

CLANCY. That happened to me a lot. Then I'd go into one of my cocaine weeks.

ROSE. Walsh never did drugs.

WALSH. Well, one night up in the Aleutian Islands, an Eskimo gave me weed—

ROSE. *(hands over her ears)* I CANNOT WORK LIKE THIS.

WALSH. Sorry.

CLANCY. Sorry.

ROSE. And stop repeating everything.

CLANCY. I just said it once. Sorry...

ROSE. We all can't work together at the same time.

CLANCY. You mean the both of us?

ROSE. Yes. The both of us.... And Walsh.

CLANCY. Walsh?

ARLENE. She didn't mean Walsh. She meant you and her.

ROSE. Stay out of this, Arlene.

ARLENE. I will. I swear. I'm out.

ROSE. *(to CLANCY)* I hear his book speaking to me. The book cries out to be finished.

WALSH. *(to ROSE)* You sound like you're making a God damn speech at Stonybrook.

ROSE. Don't you think I know where I am?

CLANCY. What do you mean? You're here.

ROSE. *(to CLANCY)* Just take notes like I told you.

CLANCY. You told me to take notes?

ARLENE. No. She told me. Not you. Sorry.

WALSH. This guy's gonna come back with a paddy wagon.

CLANCY. *(to ROSE)* Can we get back to the book? Don't you find it strange that this was the page that Walsh stopped on?

WALSH. Not in the least.

ROSE. Not in the least.

CLANCY. Why not?

ROSE. Because he was a writer. And when writers die, there's always a page they stop on.

CLANCY. Granted. Assuming even he didn't know the ending, why don't we take the book where we want it to go? Back up a few pages and go for our own ending?

ROSE. Which is what?

CLANCY. I don't know.

ROSE. Are there any other writers in Quogue who might help us?

WALSH. It's falling apart, Rose. Crumbling in front of our eyes.

ROSE. *(to WALSH)* Well, what do you expect me to do about it?

CLANCY. Well, as I suggested, why don't we back up a few pages and go for our own ending.

ROSE. I knew this would happen with you here.

CLANCY. Me?

ARLENE. No, she means...Never mind.

ROSE. We've gotten off to a bad beginning, Mr. Clancy... Why don't we call it a day. You know where the door is.

CLANCY. Is that what you want?

WALSH. Not yet. Rose. We need him.

ROSE. Maybe you do, but I don't.

CLANCY. Why do I get the feeling it's not me you're talking to?

WALSH. Don't answer that, Rose.

ROSE. I've never been afraid of the truth in my life.

CLANCY. Everybody knows that.

ROSE. Mr. Clancy, meet Walsh McLaren... Don't bother looking, you won't see him. But he's right here in the room with us.

WALSH. Jesus Christ.

CLANCY. *(looks around)* I see...Well, there's a medical name for that...

ROSE. The name for it is obsession... My obsession.... He resides in my head and soul.

CLANCY. Well, there's a name for that too.

ROSE. My nightly conversations with him are as brilliant as ever and his brains are as sharp as they were before he ate that seabass.

CLANCY. I'm sure they are.

ROSE. Don't you patronize me.

WALSH. Let him go, Rose. You've gone too far. And if he spreads the word, it will be the disintegration of a very fine woman.

ROSE. *(to* **WALSH***)* You sent for him, I didn't.

CLANCY. Actually it was Arlene.

ARLENE. I just gave the directions.

ROSE. This was a mistake, Mr. Clancy...ever since you arrived from Quagmire.

CLANCY. Quogue.

ROSE. I know it's Quogue. I was making a point.

CLANCY. And a very good point...We're all in a quagmire here...But I have an idea, Mrs. Steiner.

ROSE. Why don't you tell it to Mr. McLaren?

CLANCY. Well, I would but you'd think I was humoring you.

ROSE. I don't think there's anything you could say that I would find humorous...I think you're unqualified to finish his book. I've let this go too far. I've revealed to you something that I wouldn't even tell my own mother.

(His head turns.)

Don't look for her. My mother died forty years ago. Mr. Clancy. I would like you to leave now.

CLANCY. ...You see, I believe you see him. I believe you hear him. I envy your being able to spend so much time with him.

ROSE. Fine. Why don't you stay and work out your ideas with Mr. McLaren?

WALSH. God damn it, Rose. Stop it. You're making a travesty of this.

ROSE. *(to* **WALSH***)* It's alright. It's my travesty. *(to* **CLANCY***)* Walsh is leaving soon. Out of sight and out of my head. His attempt to secure my future with an annuity was a pipe dream, much as he is.

CLANCY. ...I didn't mean to cause a problem between you two.

ROSE. You may go now, Mr. Clancy... If you go out the beach door, you may pass him on his way out.

CLANCY. Would...would you mind if I said goodbye to him?

ROSE. Yes. This is not a ride at Disneyland.

WALSH. Say good night, Gracie.

ROSE. Good day, Clancy. And please don't tell the *New York Post* about this. They'll want pictures of the four of us.

CLANCY. You've been very kind to me... I've had a wonderful time.

(He starts to go.)

ROSE. Come and see Arlene again. For some reason I think she likes you.

CLANCY. I'd like that...Goodbye, Mrs. Steiner. *(looks around the room)* Mr. McLaren? I was honored more than you can ever know. *(to* ROSE*)* I'm sorry. I couldn't help it.

(He leaves.)

ROSE. I was not going to let him trample on our lives with a pair of filthy sneakers...

WALSH. What are you going to do for money now?

ROSE. I'll sell the copyrights to your books...They can screw up your stories on television.

WALSH. Don't try it, Rose. I can arrange for you to go sleepless till you're ninety.

ROSE. And I know where I can get pills that would put me into a permanent sleep.

WALSH. That's purgatory, Rose.

ROSE. No. These last years with you was purgatory.

WALSH. Damn you. Damn your mean selfish, twisted soul...I hate the sight of you.

(WALSH runs out.)

ROSE. Get out, you third rate amateur. *(So devastated...she looks at ARLENE.)* What?

ARLENE. Please don't sell his books to television.

(fade out)

ACT II

SCENE 1*

(Four weeks later. ARLENE *stands looking out the windows. She glances at the phone, then decides to use it. She picks up and dials...)*

ARLENE. *(obviously leaving a message)* Clancy, it's Arlene... Sorry I missed you. Yes, dinner tonight is fine...Rose told me to tell you she doesn't want to discuss the book... Better not call here...I'll call you later.

CLANCY. You don't have to.

(He is at the screen door on outside porch. She turns quickly.)

ARLENE. Oh, God... I thought it was...

CLANCY. Walsh?...Don't count me out yet...Sometimes I just look like I passed away.

(He comes in. She hangs up the phone, looks up towards the staircase.)

ARLENE. That's not funny...She's taking a nap upstairs.

CLANCY. Alone or is the big guy taking one with her?

ARLENE. That's not funny.

CLANCY. I know it's not but it's possible anyway...

ARLENE. That's none of my business.

CLANCY. How can you avoid it? You live here...Isn't there ever an extra unused toothbrush in her toilette?

ARLENE. *(looks up at stairway, then at him)* Stop it?...Please.

CLANCY. Sorry. I actually came over to tell her I did about twenty pages of Walsh's book.

ARLENE. You did? I don't know how she'll take that.

CLANCY. She'll never see it. Writing it was climbing up hill and what came out was all down hill...I know when I'm licked.

ARLENE. I'm sorry you went to all the trouble.

CLANCY. No sweat...Walsh wrote in rhythms that even Mozart would envy... And his characters are so complex, I'd have to send the book through MIT first... His title was prophetic. We all ended up in a Mexican standoff.

ARLENE. Is that the book you have there?

CLANCY. This? No. This is a sequel.

ARLENE. To what?

CLANCY. To my first and only book. Rose got my juices going again... It doesn't stand up to Walsh's but it stands up to me.

ARLENE. I'd love to read it.

CLANCY. Just the title page. I'm not ready to open the show yet.

(He hands it to her. She looks at the first page.)

ARLENE. "Death on the Patio"...Is this about Rose and Walsh?

CLANCY. Yes. In a way.

ARLENE. In what way?

CLANCY. In a specific way... Of course it's them.

ARLENE. Gavin, what have you done? She'll sue you for plagiarism.

CLANCY. Why? I'd give her fifty per cent of my profits.

ARLENE. She doesn't want your profits... Not if you reveal these last few years with her and Walsh. Don't expose the fantasies of a sick woman.

CLANCY. I never thought of her as sick. She refused to betray his work at the cost of a renewed life style for her...It's a ghost story, Arlene, with a ghost that has more charm, dignity and compassion than any walking spirit since Hamlet's father...And a hell of a lot funnier...I don't mock her. I glorify her.

ARLENE. It's her life and Walsh's after life written by her, real or not, and whatever she heard or thought she heard is her sole property.

CLANCY. I'm trying to do for her what Walsh wanted. To give her last years some comfort... Walsh's book or my book? What difference does it make?

ARLENE. Because you can't quote conversations that no one ever heard...including Rose...And what makes you so sure you'd ever make a dime out of your book?

CLANCY. Well, I did give it a sneak look at Doubledays... They offered me more fingers than I ever counted on...But I won't take it until she approves.

ARLENE. She won't.

CLANCY. I think she will... It was Walsh's last request. Now I can fulfill it...I can't bring him back but maybe I can bring back what he wanted to leave her...

ARLENE. Who said he did? Only she heard it. And she heard only what she wanted to hear.

CLANCY. She remembered the cupboard where his book was...She took it out. Whose idea was it to get it completed and make her some money?...Maybe it was her conscience that made it Walsh's idea. Maybe she's the one who put my book in his pocket.

ARLENE. Maybe...I just want to protect her.

CLANCY. That woman protects herself. If she were in the army she would be a tank...The woman has warded off everything thrown at her... The U.S. Government questioned her loyalty... Theater critics allowed her two or three big hits, then started throwing bricks at her... She hung around with an alcoholic genius who was never faithful to her... All that and not a single living relative in the world to stand up for her... Am I right about all that?

ARLENE. Except for the single living relative.

CLANCY. She has one?

(She nods.)

Who?

ARLENE. A daughter…

CLANCY. Where is she?

ARLENE. Right here…talking to you.

CLANCY. Is this a joke?

ARLENE. Do I look like a joke?

CLANCY. When did this happen?

ARLENE. A long time ago…in New Orleans… She knew her life was no place to raise a baby and the father, my father, offered to take me off her hands…

CLANCY. Why didn't she tell anyone?

ARLENE. Because it might have scandalized all three of us… "Rose Steiner's abandoned baby" and things like that…But I wasn't. I was just out on loan… She sent me gifts every Christmas and took me to dinner every birthday… We never had a mother and daughter relationship and that was fine with me…I loved my father…and she and I were friends without obligations… She probably wouldn't have made a very good mother but she became my best friend. And I like calling her Rose instead of Mom.

CLANCY. And no one knows this?

ARLENE. No one that I know. Not even Walsh.

CLANCY. Of all people, why are you telling me all this?

ARLENE. To stop you from making a fool of her in your book.

CLANCY. *(hands book to her)* Read the book. If you don't like it, I'll burn it with the rest of my unpublished offerings.

ARLENE. And if you tell anyone what I just told you, we'll deny everything you say…And I'll sue you.

CLANCY. Despite the fact that you have a crush on me.

ARLENE. What?

CLANCY. …Will you sue me if I put that in the book?

ARLENE. Probably…Can I read your book tonight?

CLANCY. We were going to dinner.

ARLENE. I can read and eat at the same time.

CLANCY. I knew there was something interesting about you... Now I see you're God damn fascinating.

ARLENE. Guess where I got it from?

CLANCY. Is it because you wanted to take care of your mother that you never married?

ARLENE. No.

CLANCY. Then why...

ARLENE. Because Walsh was the love of her life...and even though I never met him, I was looking for someone like him.

CLANCY. Even though he wasn't always faithful to her?

ARLENE. So you give up a little sometimes.

CLANCY. Would you be satisfied with that? Someone who wasn't always faithful to you?

ARLENE. Are you proposing an unfaithful relationship to me?

CLANCY. No. I already had one... Do I remind you of Walsh?

ARLENE. No. He lived in my mother's mind...You're just—

CLANCY. What?

ARLENE. Just a guy from Quogue.

CLANCY. You don't find Quoguees attractive?

ARLENE. A little...But it'll go away in the morning.

CLANCY. What if I didn't go away in the morning?

ARLENE. ...Gavin, there's not a chance in the world that you and I would–

(He grabs her and kisses her fully on the lips, then looks at her.)

CLANCY. Come around to Quogue sometime.

(He starts to go.)

ARLENE. *(dazed)* How about breakfast at your place?

(The lights dim out.)

SCENE 2*

(A few days later. **ARLENE** *is putting lunch on the table. It is a very sunny day.)*

ARLENE. Would you like some lunch, Rose?

ROSE. I'm sick of your watery tuna salad.

ARLENE. Do you want to come down or shall I bring it up?

ROSE. *(from above)* If you bring it up, I'll only throw it up... Take it away. I don't want to see it.

ARLENE. *(puts a cloth over it)* I'll put it outside for the dog.

ROSE. What dog?

ARLENE. The one who comes around every day to eat the breakfast I made for you.

ROSE. Stop making breakfast for strange dogs. We're trying to save money...Just give him a bagel and cream cheese and send him on his way.

(ROSE *slowly comes down the stairs. It's the first time we see her disheveled. A robe over a worn sleeping gown. Her hair is frizzed and unbrushed and she wears men's slippers. The sun hits her in the eyes. She puts her hand up to get it out of her eyes.)*

I told you to get rid of the sun.

ARLENE. I've tried. It persists in shining.

ROSE. Except when you want to go to the beach... Why don't you close the blinds?

ARLENE. Then you say it's too gloomy in here.

ROSE. Gloom is very popular these days.

(ARLENE closes the blind, turns on some lamps.)

Go on. Run up our electric bill. You can pay it out of your salary.

ARLENE. You don't pay me a salary.

ROSE. And you can see why.

(goes to the door to the beach, looks out)

Have any dead writers washed up on the beach?

ARLENE. Stop it, Rose. That's not funny.

ROSE. He would think so.

ARLENE. Why don't you get dressed and we'll take a walk.

ROSE. Wearing what? ...I'm selling all my clothes. I'm trying to support myself... Do I have anything you'd like...you can have it ten percent off.

ARLENE. It's not really my style, Rose.

ROSE. No. You're much prettier than me. You can thank your father for that.

ARLENE. You always said brains before beauty.

ROSE. Of course. I was hopeful that someone would believe me.

ARLENE. Let's get out of the house, Rose. You can't sit in here and mourn forever.

ROSE. I only mourn some of the time. It's the trouble with people who won't stay dead...Why don't you go see what's his name? I heard you talking to him. Francie, was it?

ARLENE. Clancy. You know it's Clancy. Stop pretending you've aged ten years in the past five weeks.

ROSE. I'm not pretending. Sometimes it's important for a woman my age to let herself fall apart. It's like a pit stop to eternity... That was good. Write it down so I can put it in my next book.

ARLENE. Are you thinking of a next book?

ROSE. I'm always thinking of one. It's better than writing one... Ask my publisher if I can sell a book I'm just thinking about.

ARLENE. Well there's another book...Gavin wrote it. I don't think you'd like it very much...It's about you and Walsh...He doesn't use your names but anyone who knows you will figure it out.

ROSE. And what do you want me to do? Sue him for libel...

ARLENE. He wants permission from you to publish the book. Doubleday offered him ten times what he made on his first book...And for your permission, he'll give you half his royalties...

ROSE. Did you read it?

ARLENE. Twice.

ROSE. Is it any good?

ARLENE. He has no right to publish it.

ROSE. That's not my question....Is it good, Arlene?...Is it prose worthy?

ARLENE. Well, he has style...Obviously following in the footprints of Walsh...I think most critics will see through it.

ROSE. Just answer my question.

ARLENE. It's not bad... But reminiscent.

ROSE. Of what?

ARLENE. "Mexican Standoff."

ROSE. How are the last forty pages?

ARLENE. Well, that's the odd thing. The last forty pages are quite good.

ROSE. Dear God...

ARLENE. What is it, Rose?

ROSE. ...Clancy's book.

ARLENE. What about it?

ROSE. Lately I've been wondering how did Clancy's book get into Walsh's bathrobe pocket...and I suddenly remembered. *(She turns and looks at ARLENE.)* ...I found it in a second hand book shop... In the mystery section... Sometimes Walsh was in the mystery section and sometimes in the literature...I would always take it out of the mystery and put it in literature where it belonged...I saw the title "Rest in Pieces," which I didn't particularly like but it sounded like a younger Walsh...And when Walsh was out of the room, I slipped it into his robe pocket.....I put it there.

ARLENE. Let's go into town. I made an appointment with Carlotta to do something with your hair.

ROSE. No. She makes my head look like a postage stamp from Lithuania...Besides, she charges too much.

ARLENE. Then I'll pay for your hair.

ROSE. No. Walsh was fond of my hair. He said my hair always looked like it was thinking. *(She looks at door again)* Come back, Walsh. Even as a Dover sole...I'll know it's you...Am I shocking you, Arlene?

ARLENE. No. I think if you talk about him, it will at least get your mind off thinking about him.

ROSE. Think before you say things like that, Arlene. Then they'll know you went to a proper school.

ARLENE. I'll accept your insults, Rose, if we can just get out for an hour. The fresh air will do you good.

ROSE. He might come back. I must be here if he comes back.

ARLENE. He's not coming back, Rose. You let him go forever. You didn't want to finish his book and now you're free, don't you understand?

ROSE. Free? You think I'm free?...I'm worse off than I was before...I'm a prisoner of his absence...for the rest of my life....If only I helped finish his God damned book...I gave away the last two weeks I could have spent with him and that's what I regret...That I cherished his words more than his presence...He was everything to me...My work and my life...When I gave him my first play to read, he looked at me and said, "Rose, that is the best damn play anyone has written in a long time"...but still made me go back and fix bad patches.

ARLENE. If the love is so real, why did you both drink so much?

ROSE. To keep the love real...A life cold sober can do terrible things to a love affair... After he died I was sitting right there... In that chair... And I prayed to God, despite the fact I was not a religious woman, that I could see Walsh again... To talk to, to be with, to have him touch me... And then I heard his voice, his rich, warm voice say to me as if nothing had happened... "What's for dinner, Rosie"...and I looked up, petrified at first... He was sitting right there, wearing this ratty bathrobe over some pajamas and these slippers that I bought him for Christmas... He returned from the dead...and what do you think I said to him?

ARLENE. What?

ROSE. I said, "What if I sent out for Chinese?"... "Just what I was thinking," he said...I was not going to question a dead man asking for Chinese food. So I decided to accept what was given to me...I would have welcomed him if he came in a bottle of formaldehyde...He came close to me and I reached out to touch him, but I couldn't feel his face or his hand...What I touched was his essence...But it didn't frighten me because I didn't want to frighten him...After all, the man might not know he was dead...So we talked all night...and we laughed...and we ate the Kung Pow with the shredded chicken and dim sum with white rice...We even had the fortune cookies. And do you know what mine said?

ARLENE. Yes. "Take what is offered to you, it may not come this way again."

ROSE. That's right.

ARLENE. The summer's almost over. Let's pack up and go back to New York...See your friends, go to your favorite restaurants...Let the world see that you're still a vibrant woman.

ROSE. I can't afford false dignity. Who would I fool? My eyes grow dimmer every day...I miss him and if he did come back, I'd have to hear his voice to know he was in the room...or smell the faint cologne he wore that cost him more than he got for a short story...He was vain you know but never conceited...There's a very delicate difference, you understand.

ARLENE. Rose, we go through this every day.

ROSE. Did I ever tell you how we met?

ARLENE. A thousand times.

ROSE. Well if it's worth telling it's worth listening to again. It was a restaurant in Hollywood. The Brown Derby. I don't know if he came over to my table or I went over to his...

ARLENE. Did I ever tell you what I did when I was nineteen?

ROSE. I shouldn't be sitting here...That's his chair...He may even be in it now...I can't see him or hear him, that's my punishment.

ARLENE. Did I ever tell you what I did when I was nineteen?

ROSE No. Why didn't you tell me when you were nineteen?

(**ARLENE** *walks away.*)

Arlene!

ARLENE. You're so unapproachable...Not even my father could get through to you...It was so daunting to talk to you...You're not someone a daughter would want to compete with.

ROSE. I never thought that's what you wanted. You should have spoken up.

ARLENE. I guess you're right. I should have spoken up.

ROSE. *(a little hurt)* It's never too late.

ARLENE. I'm thirty four. I needed you when I was nineteen.

ROSE. Alright. Pretend you're nineteen.

ARLENE. I don't want to pretend. I'll take my chances with saying what I feel now. It's bad enough that I lost all those early years with you. But when I finally get here, actually move in with my own mother, I'm shut out again...I can almost understand coming in second to Walsh...but coming in second to the ghost of Walsh is more than I can handle...And even though it's your voice I hear in your nightly conversations with him, I tend to take his side... You hold on to him even after his death because you miss him so much and still you dominate the conversations... Some nights I want to call out from upstairs, "Don't let her push you around, Walsh. She let me go when I was a child and kept you after you died"...How much control does a woman need?...Sometimes I wished he was the child and I was the one who died...At least I'd have my nights with you...I cherished all the letters you sent to me because that's all I could get from you...But it's hard to hug a letter, Rose...Especially when she doesn't sign it "Mother"...

ROSE. *(sits quietly, not moving)* ...I think that's the longest I ever let you speak without interrupting you... Tell me what happened when you were nineteen?

ARLENE. It's over, Mom...I'm not plagued by it anymore.

ROSE. But I will for the rest of my life... Please tell me, Arlene.

ARLENE. Alright...I was angry with my father because he didn't fight hard enough to keep a mother for me... So at nineteen I had an affair...He was 41...and married...with two children...I didn't think about what his wife felt, if she knew or what his kids felt... All I knew was that somebody loved me and I didn't have to wait for my birthday for someone to show their love...It lasted eight months before his wife left him and he spent all his time trying to get her back... which left me on the phone trying to find you in Paris or London or Rome... And then I heard from you..."Darling, Mother won the Pulitzer Prize today" ...And finally you came to my college graduation...to make the commencement address and at last we were together... Well at least we were commencing...

ROSE. What have I done to you?

ARLENE. You listened to me...and that's enough...

ROSE. Not for me...How do we get on with our lives?

ARLENE. Well, you can come with me and let Carlotta do your hair.

*(**ROSE** has trouble breathing and holds her chest.)*

What is it, Rose? Are you alright? ...Rose?

*(**WALSH** appears in beach door.)*

ROSE. Arlene, he's here...I can't see him... Why can't I see him? He's afraid to let me see him. He's trying to fight through but I won't let him in.

ARLENE. That's it, Mom. Fight him. Fight yourself... Don't bring him back. He doesn't have the power you have.

ROSE. Arlene, what can I do?...Help me...Talk to me. Please.

ARLENE. Maybe it really is over, Mom...Maybe it's the end of it...Maybe it's time to let Walsh go.

ROSE. It's so hard to do.

ARLENE. Don't stop talking to me, Mom. Don't look for him...Look at me. You gave more to the world than being a mother...I think you're a great woman, Rose.

ROSE. Walsh?

ARLENE. *(shouts)* LEAVE HER ALONE, WALSH...THIS IS MY TIME WITH HER, NOT YOURS...GET OUT OF HER HEAD, GOD DAMMIT. GO AWAY...

(WALSH backs away.)

(screams at WALSH somewhere) I KNOW YOU'RE DEAD, WALSH...BUT I COULD KILL YOU AGAIN...TRUST ME. I'LL GIVE YOU THREE SECONDS TO GET OUT OF HERE.

ROSE. It's alright, honey....Shh... He's gone and it's alright.

ARLENE. Are you sure? Because I could get a broom or something...I kill spiders all the time.

ROSE. Arlene, Arlene...This is our time. Yours and mine... Walsh meant no harm...He wasn't even here...I did it to myself...If you like you can publish Clancy's book... It's Walsh's gift to all of us.

ARLENE. Really? Because I think I'm in love with him. With Clancy...He's a wonderful writer, honest.

ROSE. I know...Maybe it's about time...I have to be strong now. Walsh won't understand...I've never done this to him before. *(hand to heart again)* Something's wrong, Arlene...This is not a good time for me to leave you...Call the hospital...Pack some things for me... Anything you like...Arlene, don't worry. We'll get through this too...

(go to dark)

SCENE 3

(Early evening. ROSE *comes down the staircase wearing her best robe. Her hair is combed neatly. She crosses to the porch door that leads outside. It is open. The wind blows and invigorates her. The telephone rings inside.* ROSE *turns as Arlene comes in and crosses to the phone.)*

ROSE. That's alright, honey. I was going to get it.

*(*ARLENE *ignores her and crosses to the phone and answers it. She is pleased.)*

ARLENE. Hi. I was wondering where you were...I miss you too.

ROSE. Is that Clancy? Say hello for me.

ARLENE. *(Impervious to her)* Well, I'm going to need some help with my suitcases...What good news?...Alright. I'll wait. Love you too.

(She hangs up, starts back and smiles.)

ROSE. Wait for what, honey?

(But ARLENE *doesn't respond and goes back where she came from.)*

(calls out to ARLENE*) Is anything wrong?*

(No response. WALSH *enters from the opened door on the outer porch. He is wearing an elegant gray pin striped suit, expensive shoes and a flower in his lapel.)*

WALSH. *(cheerfully)* And how are we today?

ROSE. *(turns, looks at him)* Well, well...Been to the St. Patrick's Day Parade?

WALSH. Couldn't make it...I see enough Saints where I live anyway.

(He goes to smell flowers in a vase.)

ROSE. Getting out some old duds for the fun of it?

WALSH. No, no, Rose me darlin'...I've just come from a wedding...A writer friend of mine.

ROSE. What am I doing?...You're not supposed to be here...I don't even see you anymore...Well, I do but I'm not supposed to.

WALSH. It's alright, Rose. Arlene won't see me anyway.

ROSE. I promised her it's over. I promised myself.

WALSH. Well, nothing is written in stone...except maybe hieroglyphics...Shall I tell you about the wedding?

ROSE. She may come back in. She may hear me talking to you.

WALSH. I don't think so...My friend Charles Dickens got married...Didn't write a book today so he took a wife.

ROSE. I'm not listening.

(She turns away.)

WALSH. His poor wife died two years ago so he married her sister...A lovely wedding...Herman Melville was there...Guy de Maupassant...He came with Elizabeth Browning...She came with Jane Austen.

(ARLENE enters carrying a heavy suitcase.)

ROSE. *(whispers to WALSH)* Please don't talk to me, Walsh. *(to ARLENE...)* Where are you going with the suitcase, dear?

(ARLENE drops the suitcase, then turns to go back in.)

Arlene! I'm talking to you.

(ARLENE is gone.)

WALSH. They get in moods like that sometimes...Truman Capote read part of the service...He read a chapter from *In Cold Blood*...Completely self-serving and out of taste.

ROSE. What's going on here, Walsh...You didn't come to tell me about a wedding.

WALSH. Well, perhaps not...

ROSE. I was feeling so good today and now you've spoiled everything.

WALSH. ...To tell the truth, Rose, you look tired. What have you been doing today?

ROSE. Nothing…Well, actually I was adding up the sum of my life…I wasn't very well liked, you know.

WALSH. Yes, but just by people.

ROSE. Oh, shut up.

WALSH. But, Arlene and I think you're wonderful…Despite the fact that you could have been a better mother.

ROSE. We've already settled that.

WALSH. Well, we'll see…There's always a few thunderbolts after a storm…Clancy, on the other hand truly admires you.

ROSE. He does, does he?…Tell me something…Is he for real or is he just you thirty years ago?

WALSH. Well, we won't know that for another thirty years…

(**CLANCY** *comes in from the porch*)

CLANCY. Arlene!

WALSH. The kid has good timing…

(**ARLENE** *rushes in*)

ARLENE. You rushed out so early this morning…Why didn't you wake me?

CLANCY. I left a kiss on your lips…Did you read it yet?

ARLENE. *(puts arms around his neck)* Are you in love or are you just feeling good?

CLANCY. How'd your day go?

ARLENE. It's still hard…I see her everywhere I go. Anyway, what happened at the meeting?

CLANCY. Damn good news. Doubleday wants the book out for Christmas.

ARLENE. I thought you said Christmas books get lost in the crowd.

CLANCY. I was misinformed.

ROSE. There's a reason they don't see me, Walsh… What is it?

WALSH. Young love. When you're in it, you could miss the Grand Canyon.

CLANCY. *(to* **ARLENE***)* I met with the head of the PR department...He said he cried when he read it...He said, knowing Rose, people might think the book was fiction.

ARLENE. I can understand that. Come on upstairs. I need help with the bags. I want to close up the house tonight.

CLANCY. Why not in the morning? Tonight is too good to waste.

ARLENE. I'll toss you for it.

CLANCY. I'd love to be tossed by you.

(They go upstairs.)

ROSE. *(To* **WALSH***)* What did she mean, "close up the house tonight?" What's that about?

WALSH. I'm sorry, I thought this was all clear to you.

ROSE. You're getting so vague, Walsh...I think I've outgrown you.

WALSH. Not possible, Rosie. Like two Sequoia trees we touch the sky together.

ROSE. *(looks away)* I can't understand why Arlene or Clancy didn't say a word to me.

WALSH. Good God...You really don't know...

ROSE. Know what?..... *(It hits her.)* Are you saying—

WALSH. I'm afraid so.

ROSE. ...I'm afraid to say the word...Dead?

WALSH. Or deceased...Or gone...Passed away...Demised... What else?

ROSE. I can't catch my breath.

WALSH. Well, there's a very good reason for that...You had a heart attack, Rosie...The same as I did...The result was identical.

ROSE. Why don't I feel that I'm dead?

WALSH You would if you were still alive...Well, that's not accurate. Give it some time.

ROSE. The most important event in my life and I missed it?

WALSH. Sometimes one never knows when it actually happens…You were one of the fortunate ones.

ROSE. What's fortunate about it?

WALSH Well, you sort of slipped through…

ROSE. Does Arlene know?…Well, of course she would… She couldn't see me…Poor baby…Were you there when it happened?

WALSH No. I was at my club…I was told by a friend who just passed away as well.

ROSE. Were you sad…or happy?

WALSH. A little of both…I don't mean that as unfeeling as it sounds. It's bad for you, good for me.

ROSE. Rose Steiner is dead!…How unusual for me… Exactly what time did it happen?

WALSH. Is the time important?

ROSE. Every second of life is important…Am I still in my body?…No, I couldn't be…Where is my…whatever they call it?

WALSH The loved one…as they call it…is lying at rest in Greenrose Cemetery. You'll like it…It's as green as Ireland.

ROSE. And commerce will eat it up…I'll probably end up facing a Carvel Ice Cream stand…Was there?…No. Never mind.

WALSH. Yes, a very large crowd…People drove up from everywhere.

ROSE What a thing for me to miss.

WALSH. Not really. You had the best seat in the house…

ROSE. And this house…Is Arlene selling it?

WALSH. From what I understand, they're just closing it for the winter. They'll be back next year…They think it's the ideal spot to write…

ROSE. And what about my furniture and my books and my clothes?

WALSH. Do you really care?

ROSE. Why does everyone have to give up everything after they die?

WALSH. Well, the galaxy is an enormous creation, but there's never enough closet space.

ROSE And I suppose you and I will be together for eons and eons…

WALSH. Well, maybe just one eon.

ROSE. Still have your bags packed in the hallway, Walsh?… And of course, no more writing.

(WALSH shrugs his shoulders.)

…I don't really mind laying down my pen. I didn't have that much left to say anyway… What we want to keep are the things we love most… The flowers we planted, the houses we built, the friends we made and the children we raised…or almost raised…I suppose the Philharmonic Orchestra is out of the question…

(He shrugs patiently.)

No Maria Callas?

WALSH. Booked for the next three years…

ROSE. The body goes but the vanity lingers on…Can I see what I look like dead?

(He points to a mirror, she turns.)

Oh, shit!…Oh, God, I'm sorry. Is it alright to say that. when you pass on?

WALSH. Millions have said it before you.

ROSE. Let me look again. *(she turns to the mirror)* … Actually…it's not bad…That dry skin you have as you age isn't there anymore.

WALSH. If they had a chain of stores they could make a fortune…Let's go, Rose.

ROSE. So what now?

WALSH. The tunnel is next. We all go through a tunnel that leads to a light at the end.

ROSE. Oh, don't make it sound like a Greer Garson movie…What tunnel? I don't like tunnels. They frighten me…Where is it?

WALSH. I can't describe it accurately but it looks very much like the Lincoln Tunnel.

ROSE. Are you telling me that I'll come out in New Jersey?

WALSH. Just take it as it comes, Rose.

(*CLANCY and* **ARLENE** *come out carrying a few more suitcases.*)

ARLENE. And did they settle on the title?

CLANCY. Just what I asked for. "Rose and Walsh."

ARLENE. Thank you.

(*She kisses his cheek.*)

Gavin, could you give me five minutes alone in the house? There's something I have to do.

CLANCY. Fine…I want to take some of your mother's plants with us. Otherwise they'll freeze.

ARLENE. Thank you.

ROSE. My best plants? He'll water them with Heineken beer.

(*CLANCY leaves.* **WALSH** *makes a move to leave but* **ROSE** *signals him to stay…* **ARLENE** *pours some wine from a decanter. She crosses to a place away from* **ROSE**, *sips her wine.*)

ROSE. And what about Arlene? Was I able to say goodbye to her?

WALSH. That you did, Rose.

ROSE. We lost all those years and now I've lost her forever.

WALSH. No. She'll remember you even better than it was.

ARLENE. Rose…Mother…No. Mom…This drink is to you…I love you.

ROSE. And I love you too, Angel.

WALSH. (*to* **ROSE**) Shhh. This isn't a conversation, Rose. This is between Arlene and herself.

ROSE. Oh. Of course.

ARLENE. I said some pretty harsh things to you when we had that long talk…I still mean them, not because I'm still angry…but I thought they should be said…And you let me…So here's to you.

(She sips some wine.)

ROSE. *(to* **ARLENE***)* There's a better bottle in the cellar.

WALSH. That's not the point, Rose.

ROSE. Oh.

ARLENE. It may be too late to get the record straight… But I'm proud and elated that Rose Steiner was my mother… Who wouldn't be? Please don't be angry or feel guilty when I said I missed you as a child…I'm supposed to miss you… If I didn't, what kind of a daughter would I have been? And I understand now how difficult a life it is to be judged all the time…to have to live up to expectations… If this gets too syrupy, just speak up.

ROSE. It's not syrupy at all… It's exactly what I would—

(WALSH *shakes his head at her.)*

Sorry, dear…I'm not used to playing this part.

ARLENE. …You're a loving woman…I've seen that with you and Walsh… And if I didn't get all the years with you, I got the best of them…I know you had a very tough childhood…and growing up like that deprived you of a softness…that you thought it was a weakness…it's not, Mom…I see that now…Walsh wasn't always an easy man to spend your life with…

ROSE. *(to* **WALSH***)* There. You see?

ARLENE. But he saw through your toughness… He saw the loving part of you…

WALSH. She's telling you she understands, Rose… She's giving you a higher grade than you ever got before.

ARLENE. So here's to you again, Mom…

(She sips some more wine.)

There's one thing I'm sure of… That heaven will embrace you with all it's love… And you'll be happy forever…

ROSE. Well, you have to go through the Lincoln Tunnel first...

WALSH. I said it looks like the Lincoln Tunnel...

ARLENE. I could talk to you like this for hours...but the glass is empty...

ROSE. Some other time then...

CLANCY. *(comes in quickly)* Can we go, honey. The traffic's getting heavy and I don't want to get stuck in the tunnel.

ARLENE. Goodbye, Mom. Goodbye, Walsh...Give her a kiss for me...I may call you once in a while...

(She runs out, turning the lights off. Just one light above stays on, shining down on **ROSE** *and* **WALSH**.*)*

ROSE. *(looks up)* That light never turns off.

WALSH. Come on, Rose.

ROSE. I always felt so safe in this house.

WALSH. It's not your house anymore... Come on. Give me your hand...

(He stretches his hand out to her.)

ROSE. I...I'm afraid.

WALSH. Of the cold hand of death?... I wouldn't do that to you, Rose....Just place it in mine.

(Slowly she reaches out to him and he takes her hand in his.)

ROSE. I feel it...I feel it, Walsh... It's so good to feel you again... It's so warm and comforting...

WALSH. I told you...Now blow the light out.

(She looks above at the one light on and blows...the light goes out.)

(curtain)